# Nature's Secret Adventures

## Shane Casey

### Illustrated by
## Vincent Killowry

Suitable for Dyslexic Readers

First published in 2013
Reprinted in 2016

ISBN: 978-0-9927490-0-2

3 5 7 9 10 8 6 4 2

Font: OpenDyslexic – Available at http://dyslexicfonts.com
Published by Shane Casey


Layout and Design: Shirley Casey - SLD Design

Printing: Carlow Advertiser & Printing.
Further Information: www.shanecaseybooks.ie

Quotations:
William Shakespeare - Twelfth Night
David Everett - Lines Written For A School Declamation
Roald Dahl - The Minpins

## Acknowledgements:
Thank you to all the children, parents, teachers and friends
who contributed to the editing and design of this book.

I hope you enjoy the end result

This book belongs to

....................................................

A note from the author:

Over the last three years, since we first published 'Nature's Secret Adventures', I have had the opportunity to meet with many of our readers throughout the country. Their response to Sheridan, Orla, Mervin and Maria has been overwhelmingly positive, and I am very grateful to you all... and more than a little humbled!

I hope these stories continue to inspire a love of nature, and a love of books, among all our readers, both young and old.

With best wishes,

Shane

For Mum and Dad

# The Amazing Tale of Sheridan

"Some are born great, some achieve greatness, and some have greatness thrust upon 'em"

William Shakespeare

Few pygmy shrews are ever born great, and few ever achieve greatness, but it was different for Sheridan.

He had greatness thrust upon him.

There he was, a happy young pygmy shrew, content to lead an ordinary pygmy shrew life, when something amazing happened...

Sheridan was born and raised
in the back garden of a kind old
lady. It was a wonderful little garden,
and perfect for pygmy shrews.

There was a fine hedge, full of bramble, whitethorn and roses, with violets, primroses and robin-run-the-hedge underneath.

The lawn was a carpet of daisies, dandelions and clover, with tiny tunnels sweeping through the tall grass.

There was the best of food to eat, and it was everywhere. Crunchy beetles, juicy woodlice, slimy slugs, chewy earwigs and spicy spiders!

But most importantly of all. . .
there was Cheryl

Cheryl was the most beautiful pygmy shrew there ever was.

She had beautiful little shrew eyes, beautiful shrew whiskers, and a beautiful shrew snout!

But she had no interest in Sheridan.

Sheridan wasn't the
most handsome of shrews.
He wasn't the most intelligent
shrew, or the funniest shrew,
unless you count funny-looking!

No, Sheridan was just an ordinary
little pygmy shrew, with twitching ears, a
sniffling nose and squinty eyes.

Indeed, Sheridan was the last pygmy
shrew you'd ever expect something
amazing to happen to, but that was all
about to change. . .

You see, as wonderful as Sheridan's garden home was, there was one bad thing about it.

It was also home to Terry - a big tom cat.

Now Terry wasn't an evil or malicious cat. He was just a cat, and a cat's nature is to catch pygmy shrews.

Every day, Terry would walk along the top of the garden wall, with his ears twitching, looking for something to chase. Maybe a bird, or a mouse, or even a pygmy shrew!

Most of the time, there was nothing to catch, so Terry would simply wander off to the next garden. But today, Terry had spied some movement.

Sheridan and all the other garden creatures had frozen in their places when they spotted Terry, but Terry didn't take any notice of them.

Terry's eyes were fixated on something else. . .

As Sheridan followed Terry's gaze, he realized that poor Cheryl was in real danger.

Cheryl hadn't noticed Terry. She was too busy trying to catch a tasty woodlouse for her tea.

Sheridan had to do something,
But What?

Sheridan was just a little pygmy shrew. He wouldn't stand a chance against a big tom cat like Terry.

But Cheryl was the pygmy shrew of his dreams, and he had to try something...

Suddenly, without fully realizing what he was doing, Sheridan found himself running towards Terry and squeaking for all he was worth.

Startled, Cheryl looked up from her tea, in the direction of the high pitched squeals. What on earth has gotten into Sheridan, she wondered.

But it was only when Sheridan kept running past her, still squeaking at the top of his voice, that she noticed Terry. And he was ready to pounce.

Now, what happened next will go down in pygmy shrew history. Sheridan ran straight under Terry's feet, and gave Terry the biggest fright he had ever got.

No pygmy shrew had ever dared to take on a tom cat before, and if they did, they never lived to tell the tale.

Well, that tom cat must have jumped six feet into the air! By the time he landed, both Sheridan and Cheryl had escaped into the safety of the hedge.

Terry ran straight out of that garden as fast as he could, and never bothered the little creatures of the garden again.

After his heroics, Cheryl couldn't take her eyes off Sheridan. He may not have been the most handsome of pygmy shrews, the most intelligent or even the funniest.
But to Cheryl, he was her hero.

And as for Sheridan, well, after that he was more than an ordinary little pygmy shrew. He was the happiest little pygmy shrew there ever was!

The End

# Orla's Big Day

"Large streams from little fountains flow,
Tall oaks from little acorns grow"

David Everett

Orla was very nervous. She was so nervous, she couldn't eat the delicious trout her mother had caught her for breakfast. She even turned her nose up at the eels, her favourite breakfast dish.

In fact, Orla was so nervous she couldn't even enjoy her morning splash around in the water. Now, all otters are by their nature very shy and nervous creatures. But on this particular morning, Orla had good reason to be extra nervous.

You see, it was Orla's first day at school and the first time she was going to be away from her family.

Poor Orla, she kept thinking 'is the teacher going to be nice?', 'will I make any friends?', and 'will I get lots of homework?'

Orla's mum did everything she could to ease Orla's nerves. She gave her a big hug, and asked her to be a brave girl.

She even promised to collect Orla at the end of school and bring her for a special treat.

So Orla took a deep breath, and put on her bravest face.

Orla's school was on the river bank, not far from the Holt where she lived with her family. Her classroom was under an old willow tree which overhung the river.

Oh it was magical. Its branches lazily broke the surface of the water, sending tiny ripples downstream. The leaves sang an enchanted duet with the gentle breeze.

And as the sun rose above the horizon each morning, it cast a shimmering shadow on the water.

Orla was still looking around in awe, when a friendly little duckling waddled over to her.

"Would you like to play a game with us?" quacked the little duckling.

Orla loved playing games, and very soon she had forgotten all about her nerves and had made lots of new friends.

Orla's teacher was Mrs. Teal. She was a kind old duck who spent much of her time visiting friends and relatives in Iceland and Russia.

Mrs. Teal constantly waddled over and back across the front of the classroom, recounting the many adventures she had as a young duck. She told stories about migrating across the world, and the lessons she had learned along the way.

And occasionally she got a fit of spontaneous quacking in the middle of her lesson, which brought giggles to all her students.

But Mrs. Teal was also a very wise duck.
On that first day she held out a tiny
acorn in her wing and said,
"From this little acorn,
a mighty oak will grow."

Then she smiled at her class and said,
"Now, my little acorns, tell me what
you'd like to be when you grow up."

Milly, the little duckling who had asked Orla to play, was the first one to answer. Milly certainly wasn't short on confidence.

"I'm going to be the greatest mallard duck of all time, and when I grow up, I'm going to fly all over the world".

"That's nothing," said Simon, a young salmon, "When I grow up I'm going to leave this river and swim across the North Atlantic Ocean.

Then, when I'm older, I'm going to return to this same river to raise a family, just like my parents and grandparents did".

"When we grow up, we're going to grow legs and become frogs," chanted a dozen tiny tadpoles.

"Then we'll climb out of the water to live on the land and breathe air."

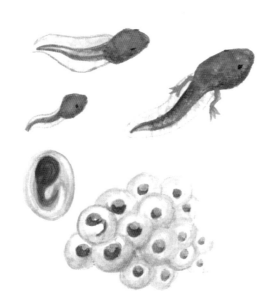

"Well, when I grow up, I'm going to leave this river as well," said Mary, a tiny mayfly larva. "I'm going to swim to the surface of the river, grow long, beautiful wings and fly away".

So each child got their chance to answer Mrs Teal's question. Every answer was more amazing than the last, and brought gasps of awe from everybody.

Finally, it was Orla's turn. Orla had never thought about this before as she had always been too busy having fun and playing games.

"I could be an Olympic swimmer," answered Orla, "or catch the world's biggest trout. On the other hand, I just love playing in the water, so maybe I'll join the circus."

At this, all the children in the class giggled, including Mrs Teal.

"I think you would be a very popular circus performer, and make a lot of people laugh and smile," said Mrs Teal.

"Well," said Orla, "I hope that I can still have fun with my friends when I grow up, but right now, I'm just happy being me".

"That's a fantastic idea, Orla," said Mrs Teal, who then announced it was high time they all had a little more fun.

So the rest of the day was spent playing games and having fun. Before she knew it, Orla's first day of school had come to an end.

And no, there was no homework that first day either!

The End

# The Fairy's Foxtrot

"And above all, watch with glittering eyes the whole world around you because the greatest secrets are always hidden in the most unlikely places"

Roald Dahl

Sometimes, legends begin as real events, but each time the story is told, the facts change a little bit, or become exaggerated. Other times, legends come from mysteries. When we search for an explanation, we take the facts we know are true, and form a story around them.

Legends capture the imagination of all those who hear them, and have been told from the dawn of time itself.

Some legends are about heroes or villains, while others are about great events or terrible disasters.

But have you ever wondered how the telling of legends began? Or indeed, what was the first legend ever told? Well, today you can find out!

Long before dinosaurs ruled the world, there were mayflies, and it was among young mayflies that the very first legend was recorded. Rumour has it, that this legend is still whispered among mayflies today.

It tells the tale of Mervin and Maria, and is known as 'The Fairy's Foxtrot'.

It is a story filled with danger, excitement, beauty and romance.
But to understand where the legend came from, we must first understand the mayfly.

You see, mayflies have a peculiar way of life. They hatch from eggs and live as nymphs for most of their life on the bed of streams and rivers, hiding under rocks or in the mud.

Then, one day in mid-summer, when the morning is still young, the wind is silent, and the air is heavy, a strange sensation comes over the nymphs.

They get an uncontrollable urge to swim towards the surface.
They emerge from the water, and sit on its surface for a few moments. It is here that something magical happens.

They are transformed into beautiful
winged creatures, known by old
fishermen as 'duns'.

Now, none of these duns will ever
return to the river bed, as they only
live for a single day. So what happens
to the mayflies, after they emerge from
the water, remains a mystery to the
next generation of nymphs.

And many years ago, when young
mayflies were gazing up at the stars
from their river bed, and dreaming what
the world would be like beyond the
water's surface, a legend was born.

So it was for Mervin and Maria.
Even though they had lived their entire
lives at the bottom of the same stream,
it was only when they reached the
surface, and sat facing each other, that
they first met.

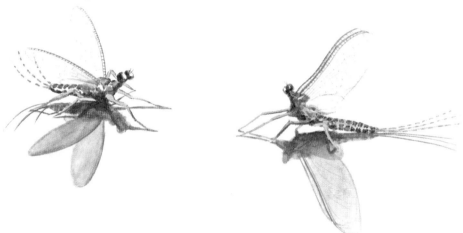

When Maria saw Mervin, she thought he
was very good-looking, even if he was
a little clumsy, as he struggled to find
his balance on the water's surface.
As for Mervin, he saw the most beautiful
creature he could ever imagine.

Maria was robed in hazel-brown, with her wings glistening in the morning sun.

But love's first tender moments were quickly dashed. Huge monsters, with wide open mouths, appeared from every side, and began to swallow up the duns.

You see, the most dangerous time for a mayfly are those first few moments when they sit on the surface of the water.

They see their new world for the first time, and feel the gentle summer breeze and the sun's warmth. Many become hypnotized by the beauty of what they see, and forget the dangers which are lurking all around.

Birds attack from the air above, while fish and frogs attack from below the water's surface. Unfortunately for many duns, they never get a chance to use their beautiful wings.

Mervin and Maria were among the lucky few.

Thousands of duns suddenly rose up from the water and began flying in every direction.

In the confusion, Mervin lost sight of Maria, and was swept along with the crowd. His maiden flight was shaky and terrifying, until he finally found a young willow tree on the river bank.

He hung onto a twig for dear life, with his eyes shut tight, as he tried to hide himself. His heart was beating fast, and he was shivering from the adrenalin pumping through his tiny body. It took quite a while, but finally, Mervin was brave enough to open his eyes, and what he saw astounded him.

The stream from which he had emerged, that had been his world for so long, now seemed very small.

It winded its way across a vast rolling countryside, with huge mountains reaching up to the stars, and endless green valleys.

There were woodlands with mighty oak trees, and lakes where wild ducks paddled happily. A blackbird was singing, while robins and finches were busy building nests.

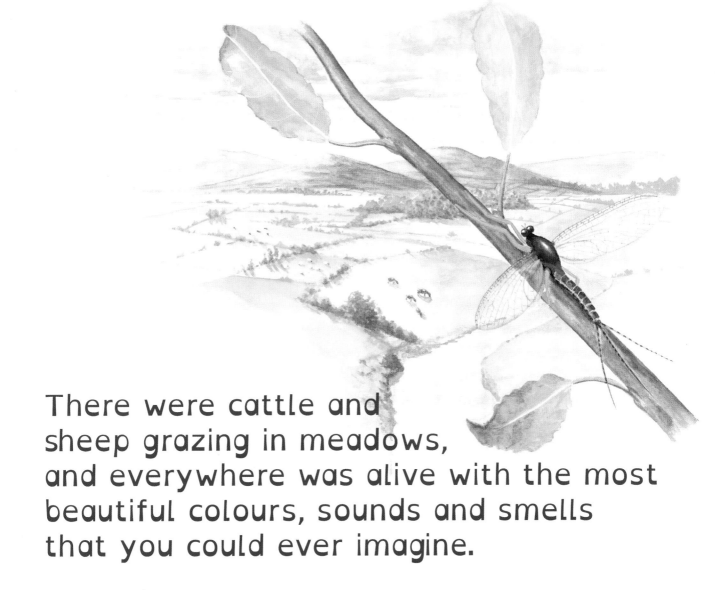

There were cattle and
sheep grazing in meadows,
and everywhere was alive with the most
beautiful colours, sounds and smells
that you could ever imagine.

Mervin watched in wonder all day, until
the dew began to fall, and the evening
shadows lengthened.

Then suddenly, he caught sight of something that shocked him. It was his reflection, in a dew drop, at the end of a willow leaf.

You see, in the amazing world of insects, there is something truly unique to mayflies. Many insects are transformed once in their lives, but only mayflies are transformed twice!

Like a ballerina being transformed into an angel, a dun is transformed into a 'spinner'. The spinners are dressed in the most vibrant of colours, with long and delicate wings.

Mervin had changed from a modestly good-looking, pale brown dun, to a strikingly handsome spinner, with a royal blue body and long silver wings.

And then Mervin saw it, just as the sun was sinking beneath the horizon. Spinners had begun to gather above the stream.

There were thousands of them, but what were they doing? Mervin watched them, and suddenly, they began to dance...

They say that this is the oldest
dance known in nature. According to
the legend, it is such a magical sight
to behold, that you would become
hypnotised by its sheer beauty.
They call it 'The Fairy's Foxtrot'.

But there was something else which
caught Mervin's eye. Among the many
thousands of spinners that were there
that night, one stood out.

She was dressed in olive-green, and
had the most beautiful and elegant of
wings. Mervin didn't recognise her, but

something seemed very familiar...
Mervin was drawn to her. Without fully
realising what he was doing, he found
himself flying towards her.

It wasn't a shaky flight like his first one
had been. This time he was swift and
graceful.

As he drew near, she became more and
more beautiful, until finally, they were
nose to nose.

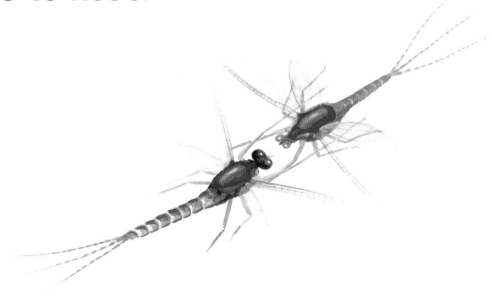

It was only then, looking into her eyes, that he recognised Maria, and she recognised him.

What happened next should not be regarded as a tragedy, but as destiny. You see, it's at the 'fairy's foxtrot' that all spinners will find a mate, lay eggs on the water's surface, and as the sun disappears and the moon climbs high in the sky, the spinners die.

For Mervin and Maria, they fell in love in a fleeting moment as they sat on the water's surface. Then, having been separated in a strange new world, it was destiny that brought them back together during one of the most beautiful scenes in nature.

And as the legend goes, Mervin and Maria danced together long into the night, as the stars gazed down in wonder.

The End

# A Little Bit About:

## PYGMY SHREWS

Pygmy shrews are Ireland's smallest native mammal, and are widespread throughout the country.

They live almost everywhere, hiding among undergrowth and leaf litter, and weigh only 4 grams, or the same as a teaspoon of sugar.

They need to eat every two or three hours to stay alive, and prefer beetles, woodlice, and flies, but they will eat almost any bug they find, including slugs, earwigs, and spiders.

They are constantly squeaking, but their squeaks are very high-pitched, and are best heard by children. So next time you are in your garden, keep a look out!

# OTTERS

Otters are one of Ireland's oldest mammals, arriving here at the end of the last ice age.

They are widespread and found along most of our rivers and streams, even in towns and cities.

Their webbed feet, long stream-lined bodies, and thick fur coats make them ideal for living in or near water.

Their home is called a 'holt', and is usually found along a river bank.

Otters are very shy and timid creatures, and are most active after dusk. But they are also very playful, and are often seen having fun on mud slides, and even playing 'catch' with pebbles.

# MAYFLIES

Mayflies are thought to have been around since before the dinosaurs, and there are currently thirty-three different species found in Ireland.

They are found in most rivers, streams and lakes, and are indicators of water quality. Mayflies are very sensitive to pollution, and so their presence indicates that the water is clean.

They live most of their lives as nymphs on the riverbed, and for only a very short time, often just a single day, as adults.

When they become adults, they do so in huge swarms, which can be seen dancing above the waters surface.